To my sister, Andy
B.B.

For Linda
A.R.

DOWN THE ROAD TO JAMIE'S HOUSE
Written by Beverley Birch
Illustrated by Adrian Reynolds
British Library Cataloguing in Publication Data
A catalogue record of this book is available from the British Library

Text copyright © Beverley Birch 1999
Illustrations copyright © Adrian Reynolds 1999

The right of Beverley Birch and Adrian Reynolds to be identified
as the author and illustrator of the Work has been asserted by them in
accordance with the Copyright, Designs and Patents Act 1988.

Published 1999 by Hodder Children's Books,
a division of Hodder Headline plc,
London NW1 3BH

10 9 8 7 6 5 4 3 2 1

ISBN 0 340 716029 (HB)
0 340 716037 (PB)

Printed in Hong Kong

Down the Road
to
Jamie's House

Written by **Beverley Birch**

Illustrated by **Adrian Reynolds**

Hodder
Children's
Books

A division of Hodder Headline plc

Annie was a bear
huge and brown and growling
padding through the snow with Jojo the baby bear
snuffling, sniffing
slosh slosh
grrrrr!

Mum was feeding Ben.
'That's fun,' she said,
feeding Ben and smiling . . .

Annie was an explorer, climbing mountains
digging snow-holes in the ice.
She said to Mum, 'Come and see.
You hide inside from
polar bears and blizzards.'

'Mmm,' said Mum,
giving Ben a drink.
Feeding Ben.
Not looking.

'You have to crawl inside,' said Annie.
'Deep inside the snow, properly.
To see how warm and safe it is.'

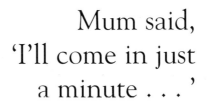

Mum said,
'I'll come in just
a minute . . .'

'Now,' said Annie,
'or the snow'll melt away.'
But Mum was feeding Ben,
not hearing.

'The snow-hole's *melting*,' Annie said to Jojo
the explorer's dog yapping and snuffling
along the snow looking for bears.
'Jamie'll dig snow-holes,' she said to Mum.
'And Jamie'll build igloos in the ice.
I want to go to Jamie's house.'
'Mmm,' said Mum, 'I'll finish
feeding Ben and . . .'

'But feeding Ben
takes hours and hours
and days and days
and weeks and weeks
and months and months
and even all the year,'
said Annie.

'I'm going to Jamie's house,'
she said.

'It's down the road and through the park
and just around the corner.
It's by the very tall tree and the big white house.'

She packed the things she'd need for Jamie's house.

Her blizzard tent.

Her explorer's hat.

Her purple wizard fingers . . .

. . . two bananas - one for lunch, and one for tea.
Her green car, and the lorry - just in case.
The binoculars she made yesterday for seeing
wild animals, fierce and dangerous,
on the way to Jamie's house.
Her lucky beads.
Her very best book
about the tiger . . .

Down the road.
To the giant park gates.
Inside.
The elephant lifted its trunk
and trumpeted hello.

Annie rode it through the dark green forest
across the raging, rocky river
to the wide, wide plains
on the way to Jamie's house.

The elephant trumpeted goodbye.

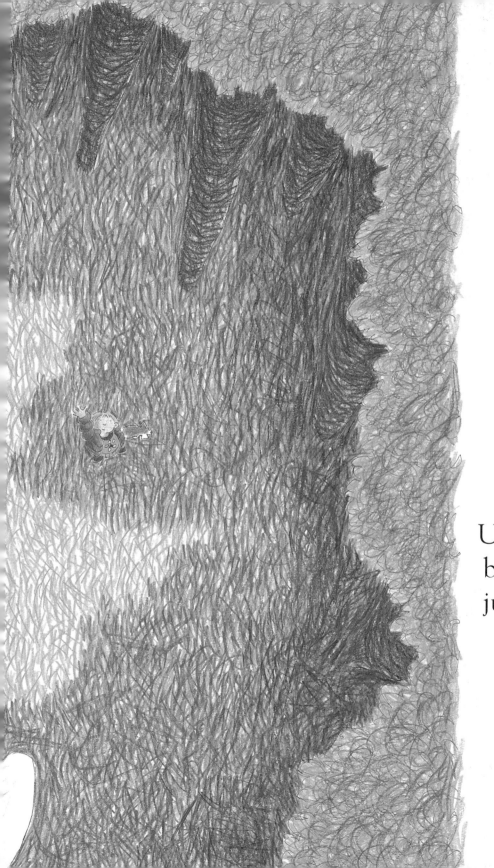

'Jamie's house is by
the trees.
Under the very tall tree
by the big white house,
just around the corner,'
said Annie,
running
quick
into
the trees.

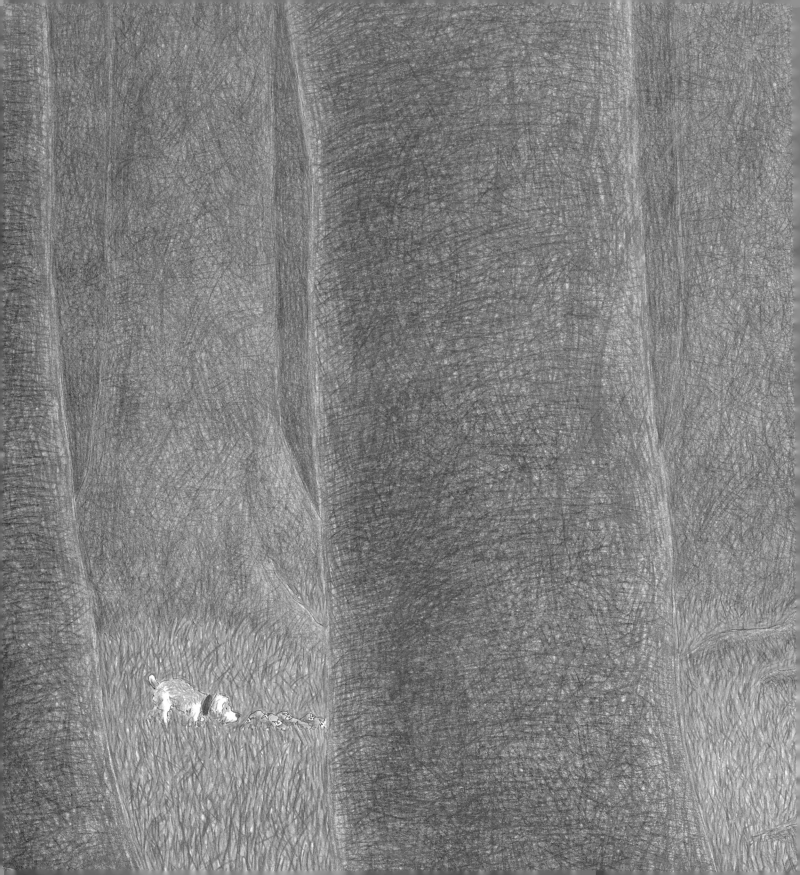

Tall trees
dark trees
whispering trees
sighing.

Split! Splat!
Raindrops
plopping
splashing
Annie's face.

Shadows crouching
hissing
in the rain.

'But Jamie's house is by the very tall tree
and the big white house . . .'
Annie stood in the drizzle and felt very strange.
Her legs were wobbly . . .

and her mouth even wobblier still,
and something kept tickling her nose
making her sniff
(though she didn't feel like crying, not for one minute).

She wanted her
explorer's hat,
but it wasn't
on her head.

And if she had her purple wizard fingers
she could make a spell . . .

No Jojo . . .
only
someone very big
and very loud
and grey rain
trickling
on a soggy tiger book.

Annie's wobbles became so big
she had to sit down
right there
and let them all come out
in tears.

'I'm going to Jamie's house,' she said.

'Annie! Annie!'

'I went to Jamie's house,'
said Annie.
'But it wasn't there.'

'Of course it wasn't,' said Mum.
'It's far away, the other side of the park . . .
I said we'd go, you know.
Why didn't you wait for me?'

'You were feeding Ben,' said Annie.
'And feeding Ben takes hours and hours
and days and days
and weeks and weeks
and months and months
and even all the year!'

'Half an hour, you mean!'
said Annie's mum.
'Half an hour!
You gave me such a fright!
Don't *ever* run away like that again.
If you want to go
somewhere, just say!'

'I did,' said Annie.
'But maybe . . .
I think, maybe . . .
perhaps . . .
next time . . .

. . . I'll wait.'